For Bryony and Leonie

First published in Great Britain by Andersen Press Ltd.

Printed in Italy

First U.S. Edition 1996
2 3 4 5 6 7 8 9 10

Library of Congress Cataloging in Publication Data

McKee, David.
Elmer and Wilbur / by David McKee, [author and illustrator].
p. cm.
Summary: When Elmer and the other elephants search for Wilbur, they have trouble finding him because his is a ventriloquist and they keep looking in the wrong places.
ISBN 0-688-14934-0
[1. Elephants—Fiction. 2. Ventriloquism—Fiction.] I. Title.
PZ7.M19448En 1996
[E]—dc20   96-3698 CIP AC

ELMER AND WILBUR

David McKee

Lothrop, Lee & Shepard Books
New York

Elmer, the patchwork elephant, was
waiting for his cousin Wilbur, who was
coming to visit.

"He's late," said Elmer. "Maybe he's
lost. Let's go and look for him."

"What does Wilbur look like?" asked an elephant.

"Wait and see," chuckled Elmer. "But be careful, Wilbur likes to play tricks, especially with his voice. He's a ventriloquist. He can make his voice sound as if it is coming from a different place than where he is—from anywhere."

"This is fun," said an elephant as they started to search. "It's like hide-and-seek."

Suddenly they heard, "Yo Ho! Elmer! I'm over here."
They rushed to where the voice came from.
"Looking for me?" asked a rather surprised tiger.
"Sorry," said Elmer, "we thought you were my cousin."
"Very funny, Elmer," said the tiger. "Maybe that's
your cousin I hear shouting."

"Help!" called the voice. "Help! I've fallen in the pond."

"He has, he has! I can see him!" said an elephant.

"Silly," said Elmer. "That's your own reflection. Keep looking. He's near, but not where his voice is."

They kept looking, but the voice kept coming from different places. "Here I am," it called, or "BOO!" to make them jump. It even came from down a rabbit hole. The rabbits popped out like popcorn. "That's not funny!" they said. "Not funny at all. That's very silly."

After a lot of searching, an elephant said, "We'll never find him, Elmer. Let's give up."

"Wilbur," called Elmer. "We give up. You can come out now."

"I can't. I'm stuck up a tree," Wilbur's voice said from above them.

The elephants giggled. "He's very clever," said one.

"If you don't come," said Elmer. "We'll have to go home without you."

"I really am stuck up a tree," said Wilbur's voice. The elephants giggled again.

"Elmer," said an elephant. "Is Wilbur black and white?"

"Yes. Why?" said Elmer.

"I peeked," said the elephant. "He really is stuck up a tree."

They all looked. There was Wilbur, up a tree.
  "Wilbur," gasped Elmer. "How did you get up there?"
  "Never mind how I got up, how do I get down?"
said Wilbur.

"I've no idea," said Elmer. "But we're hungry so we're going home for supper. At least we know where you are now. Goodbye, Wilbur. See you tomorrow."

With that Elmer started to lead the other elephants away.
"Oh, Elmer," called Wilbur. "Don't leave me. I'm starving."

"Ha, ha, I was just teasing," laughed Elmer, turning back to Wilbur. "If you walk along the branch, it will bend down with your weight and we can help you down."

Wilbur walked slowly along the branch. The branch began to bend down. When the elephants could reach it, they pulled it the rest of the way and helped Wilbur off.

"Thanks," said Wilbur. "Now, where's that supper you were talking about?" Then, laughing and joking together, they raced all the way home.

That night, as they lay down to sleep, Elmer said, "Goodnight,
Wilbur. Goodnight, Moon." A voice that seemed to come from
the moon said, "Goodnight, elephants. Sweet dreams."

Elmer smiled and whispered, "Wilbur, how DID you get up that tree?" But Wilbur was already asleep.